Dear Parent:

Congratulations! Your child is taking the first steps on an exciting journey. The destination? Independent reading!

STEP INTO READING® will help your child get there. The program offers five steps to reading success. Each step includes fun stories and colorful art. There are also Step into Reading Sticker Books, Step into Reading Math Readers, Step into Reading Write-In Readers, Step into Reading Phonics Readers, and Step into Reading Phonics First Steps! Boxed Sets—a complete literacy program with something for every child.

Learning to Read, Step by Step!

Ready to Read   Preschool–Kindergarten
• big type and easy words • rhyme and rhythm • picture clues
For children who know the alphabet and are eager to begin reading.

Reading with Help   Preschool–Grade 1
• basic vocabulary • short sentences • simple stories
For children who recognize familiar words and sound out new words with help.

Reading on Your Own   Grades 1–3
• engaging characters • easy-to-follow plots • popular topics
For children who are ready to read on their own.

Reading Paragraphs   Grades 2–3
• challenging vocabulary • short paragraphs • exciting stories
For newly independent readers who read simple sentences with confidence.

Ready for Chapters   Grades 2–4
• chapters • longer paragraphs • full-color art
For children who want to take the plunge into chapter books but still like colorful pictures.

STEP INTO READING® is designed to give every child a successful reading experience. The grade levels are only guides. Children can progress through the steps at their own speed, developing confidence in their reading, no matter what their grade.

Remember, a lifetime love of reading starts with a single step!

For Martha

www.stepintoreading.com

Educators and librarians, for a variety of teaching tools, visit us at
www.randomhouse.com/teachers

Library of Congress Cataloging-in-Publication Data
Coxe, Molly.
Hot dog / by Molly Coxe. p. cm. — (Step into reading. A step 1 book)
SUMMARY: A dog tries to find a way to cool off on a hot summer day on a farm.
ISBN 0-307-26101-8 (pbk.) — ISBN 0-375-99995-7 (lib. bdg.)
[1. Dogs—Fiction. 2. Farm life—Fiction. 3. Summer—Fiction. 4. Stories in rhyme.]
I. Title. II. Series: Step into reading. Step 1 book.
PZ8.3.C8395 Ho 2003 [E]—dc21 2002013561

Printed in the United States of America 30 29
First Random House Edition

STEP INTO READING®

STEP 1

Hot Dog

By Molly Coxe

Random House 🏠 New York

Dog is hot.

Mom is not.

Go play, Dog.

Dog is hot.

Cat is not.

No way, Dog!

Dog is hot.
Pig is not.

Oh, no, Dog!

Dog is hot.

Boy is not.

Too slow, Dog!

Dog is hot.

Sheep are not.

Shoo, shoo, Dog.

Dog is hot.
Skunk is not.

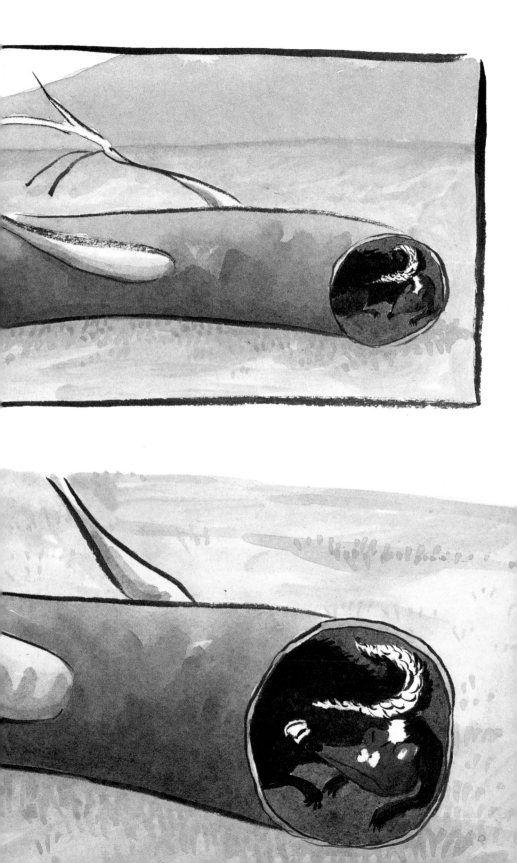

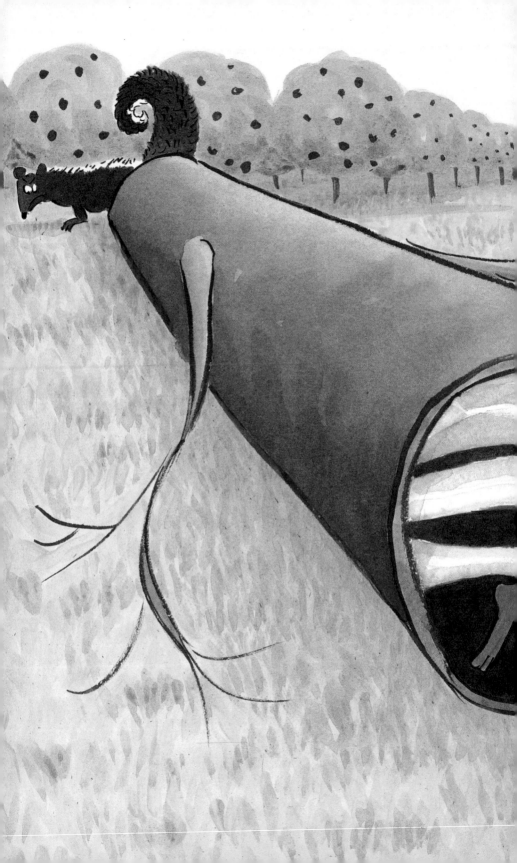

P. U., Dog!

Dog is hot.
Girl is not.

Silly Dog!

Dog is cool.

In the pool.

Chilly Dog.